S0-ANR-443

WONDER BOOKS®

Grizzly Bears

A Level One Reader

By Cynthia Klingel and Robert B. Noyed

What is big and brown
and sleeps in the winter?
A grizzly bear!

Grizzly bears are powerful animals.

They can be as heavy as 1,000 pounds (454 kilograms).

Grizzly bears are found in North America.

They have very thick, brown fur.

Grizzly bears are also called brown bears.

Grizzly bears have four strong legs.

They have sharp claws that help them dig for food.

Grizzly bears eat plants. Some eat fish and small animals.

Bears eat a lot of food. They can gain five pounds (2.3 kilograms) each day!

Word List

claws

gain

kilograms

pounds

thick

Note to Parents and Educators

Welcome to The Wonders of Reading™! These books provide text at three different levels for beginning readers to practice and strengthen their reading skills. In addition, the use of nonfiction text gives readers the valuable opportunity to *read to learn*, not just to learn to read.

These leveled readers allow children to choose books at their level of reading confidence and performance. Level One books offer beginning readers simple language, word choice, and sentence structure as well as a word list. Level Two books feature slightly more difficult vocabulary, longer sentences, and longer total text. In the back of each Level Two book are an index and a list of books and Web sites for finding out more information. Level Three books continue to extend word choice and length of text. In the back of each Level Three book are a glossary, an index, and a list of books and Web sites for further research.

State and national standards in reading and language arts emphasize using nonfiction at all levels of reading development. The Wonders of Reading™ books fill the historical void in nonfiction for primary grade readers with the additional benefit of a leveled text.

About the Authors

Cynthia Klingel has worked as a high school English teacher and an elementary teacher. She is currently the curriculum director for a Minnesota school district. Writing children's books is another way for her to continue her passion for sharing the written word with children. Cynthia is a frequent visitor to the children's section of bookstores and enjoys spending time with her many friends, family, and two daughters.

Robert Noyed started his career as a newspaper reporter. Since then, he has worked in communications and public relations for more than fourteen years for a Minnesota school district. He enjoys writing books for children and finds that it brings a different feeling of challenge and accomplishment from other writing projects. He is an avid reader who also enjoys music, theater, traveling, and spending time with his wife, son, and daughter.

Published by The Child's World®, Inc.
PO Box 326
Chanhassen, MN 55317-0326
800-599-READ
www.childsworld.com

Photo Credits
© 2002 James Balog/Stone: 21
© James P. Rowan: 6
© 2002 Johnny Johnson/Stone: 9
© John Shaw/Tom Stack & Associates: 5
© 2002 John Warden/Stone: cover
© 2002 Kathy Bushue/Stone: 13, 14
© 2000 Mary Clay/Dembinsky Photo Assoc. Inc.: 18
© Thomas Kitchin/Tom Stack & Associates: 10
© 2002 Tom Walker/Stone: 2
© Victoria Hurst/Tom Stack & Associates: 17

Project Coordination: Editorial Directions, Inc.
Photo Research: Alice K. Flanagan

Library of Congress Cataloging-in-Publication Data
Klingel, Cynthia Fitterer.
Grizzly bears / by Cynthia Klingel and Robert B. Noyed.
p. cm.
ISBN 1-56766-943-3 (lib. bdg. : alk. paper)
1. Grizzly bear—Juvenile literature. [1. Grizzly bear. 2. Bears.]
I. Noyed, Robert B. II. Title.
QL737.C27 K59 2001
599.784—dc21
00-011365